Tribune

50 cents

CTACULAR
STUNS CITY

...y involved in a massive ...rch operation after a ...h-profile cheese heists ...y.

...day asking themselves who ...d the robberies, which have ... the worst cheese shortages ...es. Detectives said they are ...open mind, but fingers are ... in the direction of notorious ... cheese thief "Fingers ...McGraw has been at large ...Valentine's Day group escape ...ways high-security prison.

... Department admit that they ...s and the only option may be to ...ctive Jumbo Wayne Jnr. out of ... to go up against the elusive ...ayne Jnr. was the detective who ...McGraw to justice over the ...Stilton" case, where an ...y rare Hartington Stilton was ...nd concealed for four months ...garden gnome. Such was the ...hock at the crime that McGraw ...tenced to 18 years in prison.

...ily *Tribune*'s ace reporter Louisa ...tracked down escaped convict ...e "Spatz da Rat" Capone to his ...own hide-out for an exclusive ...the unfolding recent events:

"Listen, dame, these ain't no nickle 'n' dime operations, see? This cat's real slick. In 'n' out quick, slippery like an eel. The law ain't got a chance!

Frankie "Spatz da Rat" Capone claims, "It's Fingers."

Lady, I'll give ya the scoop. We ain't talking no small-time hoodlum, this is the kingpin, Fingers McGraw! He's a real operator all right. He'll have made off with the loot and be aiming to stash it before the law catches up with 'im. I seen 'im nibble 'is way through two tonnes of gorgonzola in one night just to get rid of the evidence. If 'e is layin' low there's a whole lotta mouseholes around town 'e could be hidin' out in."

Police are urging the public not to approach the mouse, who may be armed and dangerous, but instead to call their local police department immediately. Cheese shopkeepers have expressed their ...and asked officials for more ...their premises.

6.00AM: THERE'S AN UNEXPECTED VISITOR TO MOO O'SULLIVAN'S CHEESE PARLOUR...

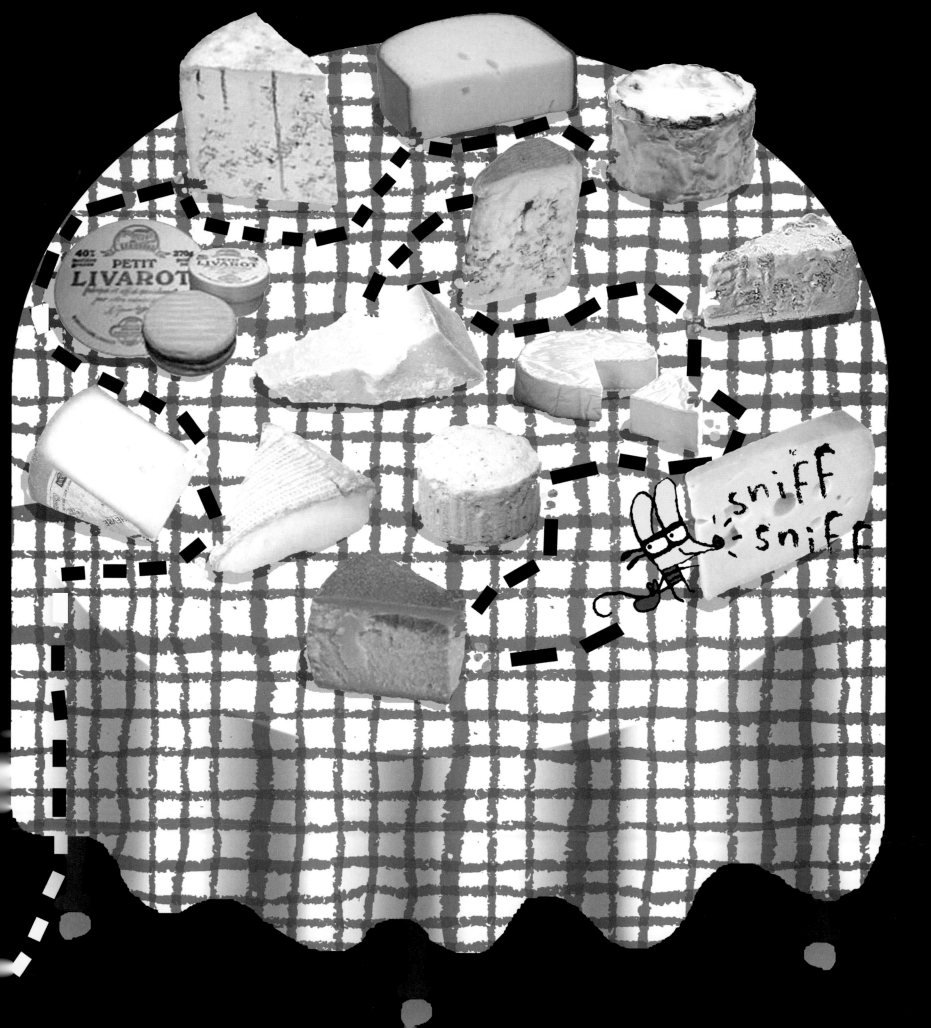

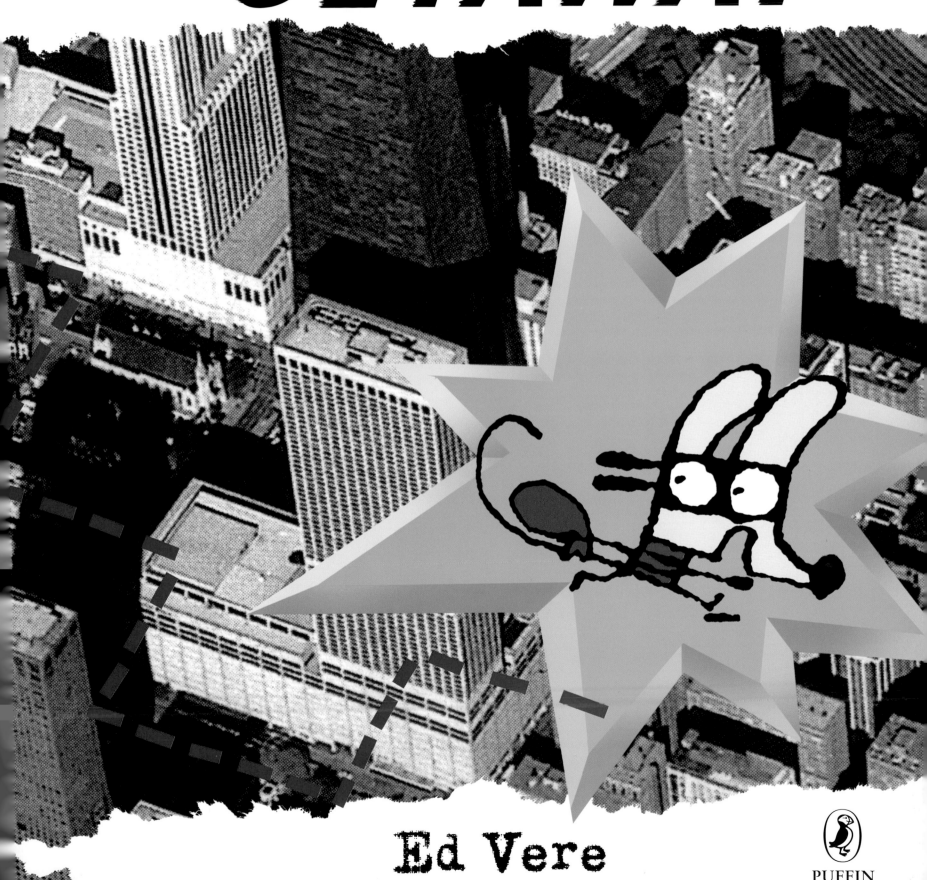

FINGERS IS ON THE RUN! BUT NOT FAR BEHIND
IS ACE LAWMAN, DETECTIVE JUMBO WAYNE JR.,
IN HOT PURSUIT!

WANTED

Cheese thief
'Fingers McGraw'
wanted for questioning
in connection with
missing cheese.

If you have seen
the Mouse
please inform
the Elephant.

Thank you

Listen kid, I'm in a fix!
I need to get rid of this cheese, fast! Be my look-out and I'll share the loot, 70/30 - OK!
Here's the deal, look out for an elephant - big eyes, big feet, big nose! If you see him, just whistle. You know how to whistle don't you? Just put your lips together and blow! OK, let's skeddadle!

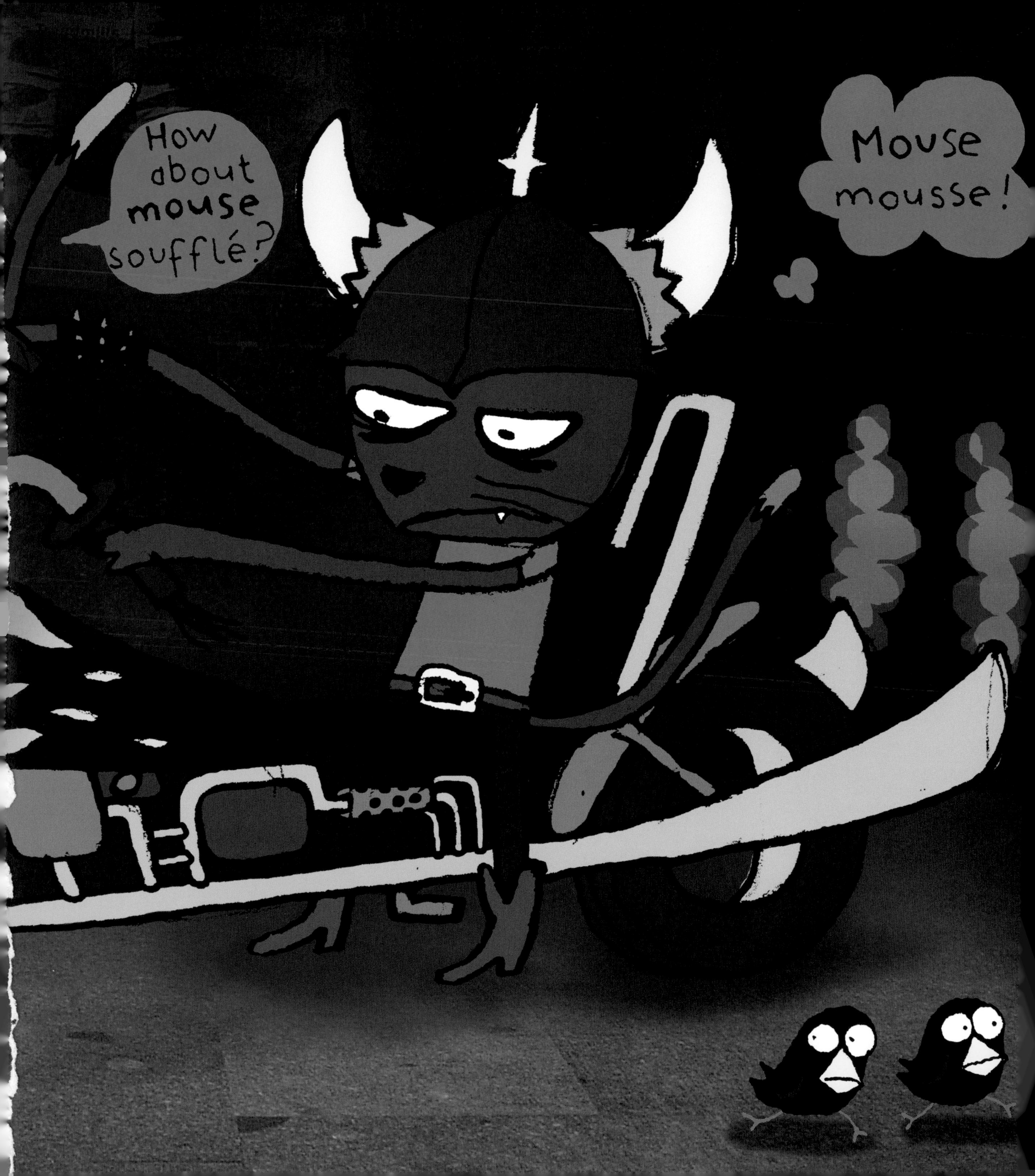
How about **mouse** soufflé?
Mouse mousse!

Mmmm, you'll taste good with a little grated cheese on top!
Pipe down boys, I'm not on the menu!
Time to disappear!

BUT WHO'S THiS?
COULD iT BE...

STOMP
STOMP

Good Grief, it's that no-good cheese thief, FINGERS McGRAW! Come back here you scoundrel!
No dice mister, you won't get your mitts on me!
?
MAP

5.00PM: THiNGS ARE HoTTiNG UP AND TiME iS RUNNiNG oUT!
Hey kid, you want a bigger cut or something?!! That was way too close! Remember, just WHISTLE!
Now,
eat
my

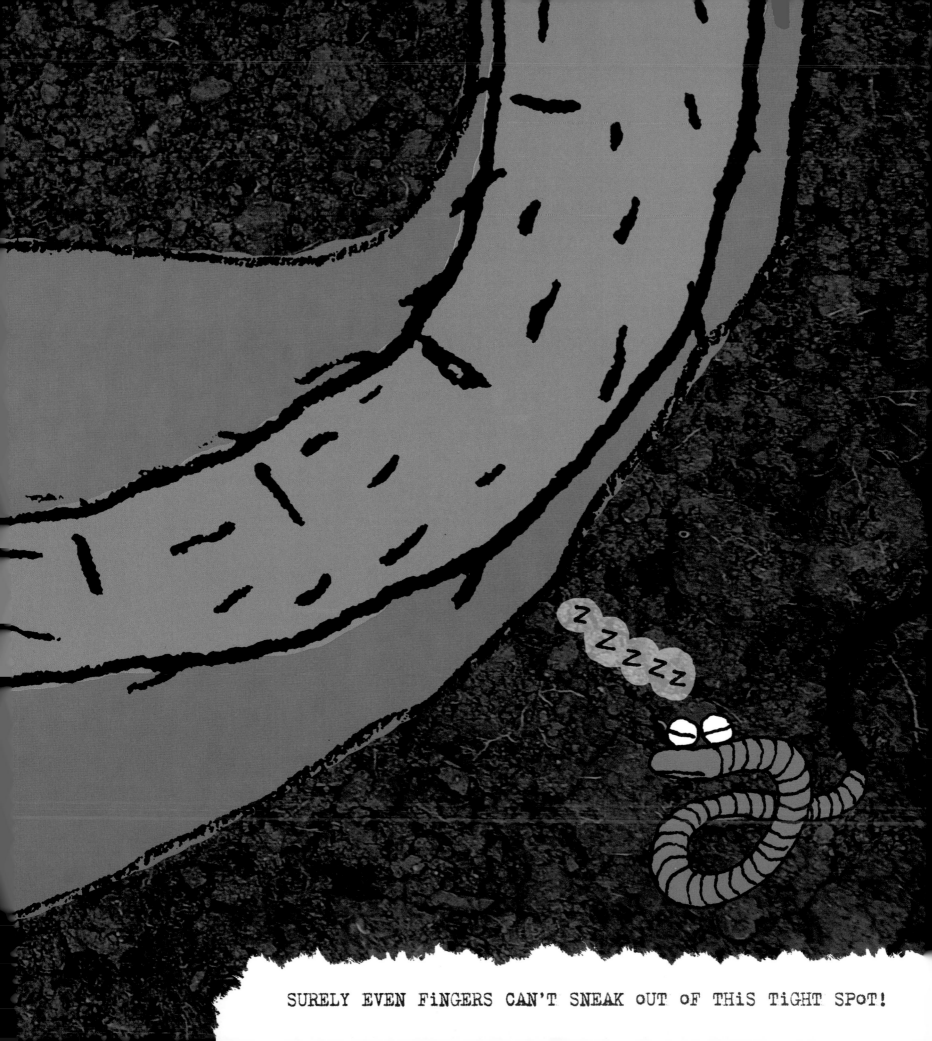

SURELY EVEN FINGERS CAN'T SNEAK OUT OF THIS TIGHT SPOT!

PH-TOOO

IS THiS THE END FoR FiNGERS...?

11.00PM: HiGH SECURiTY WiNG, MOUSEWAYS
PRiSoN. AND So WE LEAVE oUR WAYWARD FRiEND,
AT LAST HE SEES THE ERROR oF HiS WAYS AND
iS TRULY SoRRY...

...OR iS HE?

THE *GETAWAY*

PUFFIN BOOKS PRESENTS AN ED VERE PRODUCTION OF AN ED VERE FILM "THE GETAWAY"
STARRING FINGERS AS "FINGERS McGRAW" BENICIO del RHINO jr. ROMAN RATANSKI
AND INTRODUCING JUMBO WAYNE jr. III AS "THE LAWMAKER"
FILMED ON LOCATION IN LONDON, BARCELONA, CHICAGO AND BILBAO
FILMED IN MOUSE-O-VISION
WRITTEN AND DIRECTED BY ED VERE

www.edvere.com

PUFFIN BOOKS

Published by the Penguin Group: London,
New York, Ireland, Australia, Canada,
India, New Zealand and South Africa
Penguin Books Ltd, Registered Offices:
80 Strand, London WC2R ORL, England

www.penguin.com

First published 2006
10 9 8 7 6 5 4 3 2 1
Text & illustrations copyright © Ed Vere, 2006
All rights reserved
The moral right of the author/
illustrator has been asserted
Printed in China
ISBN-13: 978-0-141-38227-2
ISBN-10: 0-141-38227-9

for Bicu

The Dar

The

The DARING

The

In what is being hailed as one of the most spectacular escapes in recent memory, Fingers McGraw, the recently captured cheese thief, has managed to evade security measures at one of the world's most highly defended prisons.

Police and the prison service were left red-faced last night after it emerged that McGraw had foiled high-level security systems and fled.

Only days before, McGraw had been captured in one of the largest mousehunts the city has seen in fifty years. McGraw led the police force on a week-long "goose chase" costing the security services an estimated $500,000 a day. As well, over half the police force were involved erecting road blocks and manning air and sea ports. Detective Jumbo Wayne Jnr. had, at great expense, been coaxed out of retirement to go up against his old foe, McGraw. The detective was seen as the last resort in what was increasingly becoming an embarrassment to the Police Department, as McGraw made off with over 17 tonnes of designer cheeses from cheesemongers throughout the city over a three-month period.

In what will certainly be seen as an attempt at damage limitation, th

The *Tribune*'s ace reporter Loui again tracked down fellow convict Frankie "Spatz da Rat" for an exclusive quote.

"Listen, dan like this, see. is a smallish see and ... er, see, I'm a rat lot of cons is other creatures know, like d cats, sometimes horses. The point is these other cons is all, like, big than what a mouse is, so a mouse be smaller an' that can generally squeed out through the bars in the prison. I complicated an' that to explain, but ... well, the bars are, like, too big ... well, n exactly too big, it's the spaces betwee the bars. They is ... er ... like, too far apar The mouse, see, 'e got the knack o squeezin' out between the bars, which is too far apart, see?"

This shock revelation that the bars on the prison windows are too far apart will almost certainly lead to a far-reaching report into prison security methods and practice. Bar spacing has long been a matter for concern among the state prison community but is seen costly to "pu

Fingers

captured
the city h
had led th
'goose ch
services an
as well over
involved er
manning air a
Jumbo Wayne
been coaxed o
up against his
Detective was s

Finge
capt
the
h

have set un